Barney's™ WORLD OF TRUCKS

Written by Scott Nickel
and Gayla Amaral

Creative Director: Tricia Legault • Editorial Director: Guy Davis • Art Director: Nelson Greenfield • Additional Photography by Dennis Full

Special thanks to Freightliner LLC, Betty Garber at Highway Images, Robert Genat, Mack Trucks, Inc., Sam Parish, Ron Kimball Photography, the United States Postal Service and Yumi Ice Cream Co., Inc.

Library of Congress Number: 00-109583

ISBN: 1-58668-135-4

10 9 8 7 6 5 4 3 2 1   01 02 03 04

Printed in Mexico
First Scholastic printing, July 2001

"Trucks are everywhere! Trucks help build our homes, they bring us food, and they even take away the garbage. Come along for the ride, and let's explore the wonderful world of trucks!"

"Look at my toy trucks, Barney!" said BJ.
"Vroom! Vroom!"
"Those are super-dee-duper! Would you like to see some real trucks?" asked Barney.
"Cool!" shouted BJ.

Fire Truck

"Fire trucks are very important," said Barney. "They have loud sirens and flashing lights! Firefighters use special water hoses to put out fires and long ladders to rescue people. Sometimes they even rescue kitty cats from trees!"

PARAMEDIC ENGINE CO.

FIRE · RESCUE

Garbage Truck

"Garbage trucks help keep neighborhoods clean by picking up trash," said Barney. "Workers put the trash in the truck where it's squished and squeezed together to make room for more garbage. When I hear the garbage truck coming down the street, I know it's time to clean up!"

Car Carrier

Honk! Honk! "A car carrier is a very big truck that carries lots of cars," explained Barney. "It moves new cars from the factory to the car dealer where they're sold. Do you know how the cars get on the carrier? They drive up on special ramps."

Tow Truck

"Tow trucks are helpful," said Barney. "When cars break down, tow trucks take them to be repaired. When people see their bright, flashing lights, they know help is on the way!"

Dump Truck

"I really like to watch dump trucks work!" exclaimed Barney. "People who build things use them to carry rocks and dirt. When the driver uses special controls, the back of the truck tilts up, and the rocks and dirt come tumbling out!"

Cement Mixer

"Cement trucks make concrete for streets, parking lots and buildings," said Barney. "The mixer turns sand, cement, water, and gravel 'round and 'round until the mix is just right. Then the concrete is poured from the back of the truck. Don't walk on it until it's dry!"

Milk Truck

"Tanker trucks carry milk from the dairy where the cows are milked," said Barney. "The tank is refrigerated to keep the milk nice and cold. It must take a lot of cows to make that much milk!"

Logging Truck

"Logging trucks are very long," explained Barney. "When trees are cut down, the logs are stacked in the truck that takes the logs to the lumber mill. Hmmm! I think these logs are a little too big for my fireplace!"

Bulldozer

"Bulldozers are funny-looking trucks," laughed Barney. "Construction workers use them to clear away dirt and rocks. They're strong enough to move big boulders and lift heavy loads. That shovel can make a really big hole!"

Farm Truck

"Long ago, farmers used these trucks to carry animals and crops," said Barney. "This truck is more than 75 years old! Trucks certainly have gotten bigger since then!"

Cattle Truck

Moo! Moo! "It sounds like a tractor-trailer truck is *mooo*-ving down the road," chuckled Barney. "Some tractor-trailer trucks carry cattle. The cows ride in the trailer behind the cab. Look at all those wheels! How many can you count?"

Vehicle photograph © Bette S. Garber

Mail Truck

"I love to see the mail truck driving down the street!" exclaimed Barney. "Mail trucks deliver letters and packages from the post office to people's homes and businesses. It's always fun to get mail!"

UNITED STATES
POSTAL SERVICE

Pickup Truck

"People drive pickup trucks in the country and in the city," continued Barney. "Pickups have a cab in front where the driver sits and a handy flat area in the back to carry things. Do you know someone who drives a pickup truck?"

Ice Cream Truck

Ring-a-ling! Ring-a-ling! "This is one of my favorite trucks!" said Barney. "It drives through the neighborhood with yummy treats to eat!"

"Yahoo! It's the ice cream truck!" shouted BJ.

"Hop on board, BJ!" exclaimed Barney.
"Let's go for a ride in this 18-wheeler."
"Awesome!" shouted BJ. "I've never
been in a truck like this before!"

Vroom! Vroom!

Milk Truck

Dump Truck

Cement Mixer

Mail Truck

Fire Truck